Goldie  Blox®

GOLDIE BLOX
AND THE HAUNTED HACKS!

To the awesome students and staff at Piney Grove Elementary —S.M.

Copyright © 2018 GoldieBlox, Inc. All rights reserved. Published in the United States by Random House Children's Books, a division of Penguin Random House LLC, 1745 Broadway, New York, NY 10019, and in Canada by Penguin Random House Canada Limited, Toronto. Random House and the colophon are registered trademarks of Penguin Random House LLC. GoldieBlox and all related titles, logos, and characters are trademarks of GoldieBlox, Inc.

Visit us on the Web!
rhcbooks.com
GoldieBlox.com

Library of Congress Cataloging-in-Publication Data
is available upon request.
ISBN 978-0-525-57777-5 (trade) — ISBN 978-0-525-57779-9 (lib. bdg.) —
ISBN 978-0-525-57778-2 (ebook)

Printed in the United States of America
10 9 8 7 6 5 4 3 2 1

GOLDIE BLOX AND THE HAUNTED HACKS!

Written by Stacy McAnulty
Illustrated by Lissy Marlin

Random House 🏠 New York

THE WORK-TOGETHER MOBILE

"*T*a-*dum!*" Goldie Blox and her dog, Nacho, pulled a blue tarp off her latest invention. "I call it the work-together mobile."

Her best friends stared at the vehicle. It had ten bike seats, and each had a set of pedals. A cooler was wedged in the back. There was a single steering wheel next to the front seat.

"Did you name it the work-together mobile because we helped you build it?" Ruby Rails asked.

"Exactly!" Goldie smiled. "I couldn't have

done it without my Gearheads."

"But why the big reveal?" Li Zhang asked. He lived next door to Goldie and was used to her zany inventions.

"We just saw it yesterday," Val Voltz added.

"But you didn't see this." Goldie pressed a button on the steering wheel. A large canopy sprang up from the center. It shaded the seats, and it had a sign attached: BLOXTOWN TOURS $1.

"Awesome! Let's take it for a spin," Li said. He hopped onto a seat in the back row. Nacho jumped onto the seat next to him.

Val tilted her head. "Goldie, are you sure it's safe?"

"I'll get some safety gear," Goldie offered. She ran into the BloxShop, which was her garage filled with anything and everything the Gearheads needed to create and engineer. When she returned, she handed out helmets to her friends and Nacho.

Val slowly raised her helmet. Suddenly, she screamed and threw it down to the ground.

"What's wrong?" Goldie asked. She grabbed her friend's hand.

"There . . . was . . . a . . . bug. . . ." Val couldn't catch her breath.

Ruby picked up the helmet and pulled out the *scary* bug.

"You mean this?" she asked. "This ladybug?"

Val put her hands to her heart. "I thought it was a tarantula." She sighed. "I just don't like any bugs. They're creepy and crawly and make me shiver."

"Obviously," Ruby said, handing Val her bug-free helmet.

"Sorry. Lots of things scare me," Val said. "Bugs, rodents, some dogs, all bears, Sasquatch, pop quizzes. I tried to make a list once. I ran out of paper." She shrugged.

"Don't apologize. We're all afraid of something." Goldie hugged Val. "Come on. Let's take the WTM for a spin. Maybe we'll find someone who wants to go on a tour."

Goldie grabbed the driver's seat. Ruby and Val sat in the row behind her. Li and Nacho worked the back. They only had to pedal two blocks before they found their first customers.

Two women and one little boy each paid a dollar for a Bloxtown tour. They were given helmets. And because there were three paying customers on board, Goldie obeyed the speed limit. Mostly.

"That's my old school." She pointed over her shoulder. "I accidentally blew the roof off. But we converted it into a smoothie shop. Best maple-cheese-berry smoothies in town."

"You can also get normal flavors," Ruby whispered.

Everyone pedaled while Goldie steered. She took them up and down the streets of Bloxtown. Her helmet had a built-in microphone so she could be heard as she told the history of her hometown and pointed out local attractions.

"That's the town dump. You can find a lot of buried treasure in there. Most of the parts on this vehicle came from that dump."

One woman immediately let go of her handles and pulled out a small bottle of hand sanitizer from her purse.

Goldie laughed. "Don't worry. We cleaned them all."

The tour weaved through town. They stopped briefly to take pictures, and Val gave the customers bottles of water from the cooler.

"Why didn't we think to put a motor on this thing?" Ruby said, breathing hard.

"This is better for the environment. It's good exercise. And I promised my dad I wouldn't borrow the motor from the washing machine today because he has a couple of loads to do." Goldie flashed a big smile. "Besides. When we work together, we can do anything."

They pulled up to their last stop of the tour.

"Ladies and gentleman, on your left is the famous Bloxtown Inn." Goldie pointed at the once-white building that was now the color of dirt, and surrounded by weeds. "It's no longer open, but it's still totally cool. If you ever get a chance, I recommend trespassing. The dumb-waiter alone is worth it."

"A *dumb* what?" the little boy asked.

"A dumbwaiter. It's like a small elevator that's operated by hand. It was used to move heavy items or meals from one floor to another. Waiters wouldn't have to carry plates up and down the stairs. You should check it out."

"But be careful," Val added, "because the inn is haunted."

Goldie laughed. "Val likes to joke around. It's not haunted. There's no such thing as ghosts."

"Tell that to my great-great-uncle Reginald,"

Val replied.

"Is he a ghost?" Li asked.

"No. He's just really into spooky stuff. He has seen the ghosts at the inn. So have I."

"No way," Goldie said.

"Yes way! It's the most haunted place in town. It's haunt-a-riffic." Val pumped her fist.

"Are the ghosts friendly or dangerous?" one of the women asked.

Val waved her hand back and forth. "Somewhere in the middle."

"There are no ghosts," Goldie said again. "It's just a cool, creepy old building."

"Not for long," Ruby said. "Look. It's going to be destroyed." She pointed to a sign wedged into the bushes. The Bloxtown Inn was scheduled for demolition next week.

"That'll be awesome." Li rubbed his hands together. "I wonder if they'll use dynamite and

make it implode. That's like exploding but inward. Or if they'll use a giant bulldozer."

"No, they can't!" Goldie protested.

Li shrugged. "You're right. A bulldozer is probably too small for a three-story building. Maybe a wrecking ball."

"They can't use a wrecking ball, dynamite, or a bulldozer." Usually, Goldie would love to see a demolition using any of these three methods, but not on the inn.

"This is a landmark," Ruby added.

"Not only that," Goldie continued. "It was way ahead of its time. The contraptions and the gadgets and the—"

"Ghosts!" Val interrupted.

Goldie shook her head. "Ghosts or no ghosts, we cannot let the town destroy this building."

"You're right, G," Li said.

Goldie set the brake and then hopped off

her seat. She motioned for everyone to follow.

"Is the tour over?" the lady with the hand sanitizer asked.

Goldie grinned. "Nope, it's just getting to the good part."

PROBABLY JUST THE GHOST CAT

"This is not what we signed up for," said the woman. She and the other customers climbed off of the tour bike and headed down the street.

Goldie waved goodbye. "Thank you for trying Bloxtown Tours. Tell your friends."

The Gearheads and Nacho followed Goldie to the front porch of the Bloxtown Inn. She tried the large front doors. The place was locked tight.

They went around the building. Li pulled on the back door. Val and Goldie pushed on each window. No luck.

"Maybe we could climb to the roof and slide down the chimney," Li suggested.

"Wait. Look!" Val pointed to the storm cellar door. It hung open.

"Let's go," Goldie said.

"I guess we're just going to ignore the No Trespassing signs." Ruby scowled.

Val laughed. "That sounds like something I would say." She hooked arms with Goldie and set off for the open door.

"So," Goldie whispered to Val. "You're afraid of bugs and rats and heights and lots of other stuff, but not ghosts?"

"Of course not. I love ghosts!" Val exclaimed. Goldie gave her a puzzled look.

The door creaked as Val pulled it completely open. A cloud of dirt greeted them and they coughed. The Gearheads waved their arms to clear the air.

Nacho took a step back.

"Come on, boy." Goldie pulled a small flashlight from her hair. Her blond curls were like a toolbox. She also had a pencil, ruler, screwdriver, and compass in there. Ruby used her minicomputer for even more light.

Val led the way under the inn. "I've never been down here."

Old barrels and wooden boxes filled the rectangular room. Cobwebs and dust covered everything. As the Gearheads walked, they left fresh footprints in the dirt.

Goldie shined her light at the stairs that led up and into the inn. A door at the top had three deadbolt locks and a large padlocked bar across the middle. They still couldn't get into the main building.

Suddenly, a small animal raced out from

behind a crate. It brushed Val's leg as it ran out
the door. But she didn't jump or scream.

Nacho barked and covered his eyes with
his paws.

"What was that?" Ruby asked. She pointed
at Val. "And why didn't it scare you?"

"It was probably just the ghost cat," Val said
calmly. "We've met before."

"Wait! What?" Ruby shook her head.

"I met the ghost cat when I was little," Val explained. "Do you want to hear the story?"

"That wasn't a ghost cat," Goldie mumbled. "It was a squirrel or a raccoon." She looked around, but the critter was gone.

"I've got to sit down for this." Ruby took a seat on the edge of a crate. Li kneeled on the ground and pulled Goldie down next to him. Nacho crawled into her lap.

"I was only four or five," Val started. "My great-great-uncle had been telling me about the ghosts at this inn for as long as I could remember."

"So you were on the lookout for ghosts?" Goldie interrupted. "You came here on a ghost hunt."

"Not exactly. I came for tea with my grandma and my mom. The restaurant on the main floor used to serve high tea every afternoon. You could get a cup of Earl Grey and some delicious scones with jam and cream."

"I don't know what a scone is, but you're making me hungry." Li rubbed his stomach.

"A scone is like a biscuit or a cookie," Val explained. "I must have drunk a gallon of tea, and I needed to use the bathroom. I told my mom that I was old enough to go alone. Drinking tea in fancy china made me feel very grown up.

"I walked down the hall, found the restroom, and did my business. I washed my hands, and when I turned for a towel, a cat was sitting at my feet. He was white and—"

"There are plenty of white cats," Goldie interrupted. "Just because it was white doesn't mean it was a ghost."

"I know it was a ghost, because it was also kind of see-through and just appeared

out of thin air."
Val opened her
hands as if doing
a magic trick.

"Couldn't the cat
have snuck in with you or gone under the
door?" Ruby asked.

"No. It was a small bathroom. And not the
kind that has stalls. There was a toilet, a sink,
and a ghost cat."

Li leaned forward on his knees. His eyes
focused only on Val. "Did the cat say anything
to you?" he asked, completely serious.

"No. It's a cat. It can't talk."

Li shrugged. "It was a ghost cat. There
might be different rules for the ghost world.
Maybe animals talk and fly." He stared at Val
again. "Did he fly? Ghosts fly, right? They don't
experience gravity like we do."

"No one experiences gravity like you do," Goldie teased her friend. He was known as Li Gravity Zhang because no height was too high and no challenge was too big.

"I didn't see the cat fly. He just stared at me. I tried to pet him, but he jumped out of the way. But it was faster than a jump. It was like he transported from one spot to another." Val's eyes were huge in the dim light. Goldie could tell she really believed she'd seen a ghost cat.

"Then someone knocked on the door," Val continued. "And the ghost cat vanished into thin air. When I walked back to the table, I stopped a waiter in the hall. I said, 'Excuse me, sir, there's a cat in the bathroom.' He froze and asked me if the cat was white and fluffy. When I said yes, he dropped a tray of scones."

"What a waste of food." Li's stomach grumbled.

"The waiter told me that it was a ghost cat, and people only saw it right before something terrible was about to happen. That poor waiter was shaking all over."

"Did something terrible happen?" Ruby asked. She was shaking a little, too.

"He did drop the tray of scones," Val said.

"That's not exactly something terrible," Goldie added.

"It is if you're hungry." Li rubbed his stomach again.

"I don't remember anything terrible happening that day. But I did see a ghost cat. You believe me, right?"

Li nodded, and Ruby shrugged.

Val turned to Goldie. "You believe me, right, Goldie?"

"Um . . ." Goldie hesitated.

"Do you think I'd lie to you? You're my best

friends." Val's voice wobbled.

"I don't think you're lying on purpose," Goldie said quietly. "But ghosts aren't real."

"You weren't there." Val's face grew red. "I know what I saw."

"Let's just focus on saving the inn. Okay?" Goldie got up and put a hand on Val's shoulder.

"I guess," Val whispered.

HOMELESS GHOSTS

The next day, Goldie, Li, and Ruby headed to the town hall to fight for the old inn. But they needed to make one stop first.

Goldie pressed the Voltzes' doorbell.

Val opened the door. "Hey."

"We need you, Val," Goldie said. "We're going to talk to the mayor and the town board. We need to convince them to save the inn."

"Didn't we try to convince the mayor of something before? To reopen your old school?" Val asked. "That didn't end well."

Goldie remembered. She had accidentally kidnapped the mayor by snaring him in a net.

"This is different," Goldie promised.

"What's in the bag?" Val pointed to Goldie's backpack.

"Nothing crazy. No net cannons. We're just going to talk. Mostly. And we need you there."

"You can tell them about the ghost cat," Li said.

Val looked at Goldie. "But you don't believe me."

"That's not important," Goldie replied.

"It is to me." Val kept her eyes locked on Goldie.

"What we need is for the board to believe you." Goldie forced a smile. "With your help, we can save the inn. It's the ghost cat's habitat, after all."

If it even exists, she thought.

"Okay," Val finally agreed. "But before this is all over, I'm going to prove to you that the ghost cat is real."

Goldie and Li hopped on their souped-up skateboards. Val and Ruby took their bikes. As they rode to the town hall, Goldie imagined how she could persuade the mayor to save the inn. She could convince Nacho to do what she wanted with a strip of bacon. She wondered what meat the mayor liked.

The Gearheads parked their rides, went inside, and quietly made their way to the mayor's office.

"Knock, knock," Goldie said, standing in the open doorway. "Hello, Mayor Zander."

The mayor groaned. "What do you want?"

"Not much. Just to save the old Bloxtown

Inn." The Gearheads stepped inside the office, even though they weren't officially invited.

"It's a historic landmark," Ruby added.

The mayor smiled. Goldie noticed it wasn't his usual evil smile.

"It's scheduled for demolition next week," he said. "The town board has already made its decision."

"Well, then—we need to talk to them." Goldie took a seat in one of the leather chairs across from the mayor.

"Are you refusing to leave unless you get to talk to the town board?" Mayor Zander asked.

She shrugged. "Sure."

Mayor Zander picked up his phone and ordered someone on the other end to gather the town board.

Goldie leaned over to her friends. "This is going pretty well so far. I don't even need plan B." She patted her backpack.

Ruby stepped back. "What's plan B?"

"A tickle-machine prototype. It almost works."

Soon, the mayor's office was crowded with people in suits.

"What's going on?" asked a woman with red hair.

"What's the emergency?" asked a man with very little hair.

Goldie stood on her chair. "We're here to save the Bloxtown Inn."

"Why?" asked a man with a bow tie. "It's abandoned."

"And that land is valuable," added a woman in a green suit. "We're going to turn it into a gas station."

"It's not abandoned," Val said. "Ghosts live there. You'll be destroying their home."

The room suddenly grew quiet. Li nodded, but everyone else seemed to be frozen.

"Where do you expect the ghosts to go if they're homeless?" Val asked.

"Maybe they'll have to live here," Li said. "You've got lots of room in this building."

"This is ridiculous," the red-haired woman said. "The inn is not haunted. It's simply an eyesore."

"I don't know." The bald man shook his head. "My father used to tell me stories about the ghosts of the inn. He claimed to have seen them in the windows."

The mayor and the town board continued to argue about whether the inn was haunted and ghosts were real. Goldie did not join in. She definitely had an opinion, but she also had an idea.

She pulled a whistle from her hair and blew

it loudly. That got everyone's attention.

"None of us know if the inn is actually haunted," she said.

Val made a small *harrumph* sound.

"But if it is, can we agree that it must be saved?" Goldie looked at each board member and then at the mayor.

"Well, if it is haunted, I don't see how we could tear it down," Mayor Zander said.

"Seriously?" Ruby asked. "You'd tear down a child's playground to put up a parking lot if it meant making money."

"I don't mess around when it comes to ghosts." He crossed his arms over his chest.

"This is foolish talk," said the woman in the green suit.

"I have to agree with the mayor," the bald man said. "I don't want to upset any ghosts. They might haunt *us*."

Goldie couldn't believe what she was hearing. *Are adults afraid of ghosts?*

"You're making the right decision," Val said with a satisfied smile.

"It's not haunted!" The red-haired woman stomped her foot.

"It is!" Val snapped back.

"It's not."

"It is."

"It's not."

"It is!" Goldie interrupted. "We'll prove it. And when we do, you have to promise not to tear it down."

Val smiled. And Goldie felt bad. She didn't actually think the inn was haunted.

"If these kids can prove the inn is haunted," Mayor Zander said, "then I will declare it a Bloxtown landmark."

Goldie held out her hand. "Let's shake on it."

The mayor agreed, and the Gearheads left his office.

In the hall, Li pulled Goldie aside. "You don't believe in ghosts. You don't believe it's haunted," he whispered.

"But I can engineer that," Goldie said with a wink.

FUNNY FRED, THE CHEF, AND THE LADY IN PINK

Goldie stood at the whiteboard in the Blox-Shop. Ruby, Val, and Li crowded together on an old couch.

"We need a plan to haunt the inn," Goldie said.

"We really don't," Val said for the millionth time. "It's already haunted."

Goldie let out a loud sigh. "Well, we need a plan to make sure it seems haunted in case the ghost cat is feeling shy on Saturday night."

"He's not the only ghost there," Val mumbled.

Ruby used her minicomputer to find a blue-print of the building. Goldie drew the three floors on the whiteboard in blue marker.

"Here." Val used a red marker to show where she'd seen the ghost cat years ago.

"The town board isn't going to take our word that the inn is haunted, so we'll need cameras." Goldie drew X's where she planned to set up her equipment.

"Hey, Gearheads," Ruby said. She turned her minicomputer so they could see the screen. It showed an image search result for the Blox-town Inn. "Doesn't this look like Zeek Zander?"

They examined the old black-and-white picture. There was no way it could be Zeek. He was their classmate *now*. He was not a fan of the Gearheads and constantly caused them trouble. But the boy on the screen did look a lot like him. He stood in front of a homemade

 lemonade stand and wore a suit and a huge bow tie. He was selling drinks for five cents a glass.

"Weird," Li agreed. "Do you think Zeek's like a vampire and doesn't age?"

"You've seen him age," Ruby answered. "You've known him since kindergarten."

"Right." Li nodded.

Ruby continued looking at pictures of the inn online. "All sorts of famous people have stayed at the inn," she said. "Movie stars, the governor, astronauts, fashion designers. The list goes on and on."

"I wonder why they closed it down," Goldie said out loud.

"Maybe because it's haunted." Val turned to

Ruby. "Look it up."

Ruby tapped on her minicomputer. Then she read to them about the history of the building.

"It was constructed over one hundred years ago," she began. "That's before Bloxtown was even called Bloxtown. It was just *The Inn* back then. When it was first built, it didn't have electricity. But it did have a dumbwaiter."

"Which I've ridden in," Goldie said.

"And laundry chutes," Ruby continued.

"Which I've slid in," Li added.

"And automatic doors." Ruby tapped her minicomputer.

"How could it have automatic doors without electricity?" Val asked.

"They didn't automatically open like the

doors of a grocery store do today. They're much, much cooler." Goldie jumped up on the workbench to explain. "The double doors in the dining room are automatic. If you close one, the other also closes because they're tied together under the floor with chains and pulleys. Simple, yet awesome!"

"Are you sure it's not ghosts?" Ruby asked.

Goldie rolled her eyes. "Not you, too, Rubes." She crawled off the workbench.

"No, I'm serious," Ruby said. "There are dozens of reports about ghost sightings."

Val sat up and clasped her hands in excitement.

"It says here that there is a comedian named Funny Fred who haunts room twenty-seven. People have heard him saying 'knock knock' and laughing over and over again." Ruby's face lost all color. "And he likes to make farting sounds in the bathroom."

"That's frighteningly funny," Goldie said.

Ruby continued. "And there's Chef, who hangs out in the kitchen. The former staff reported weird things happening, like dishes falling off shelves and the faucet turning on all by themselves."

"But was Chef a good cook? Could he make waffles?" Goldie asked.

"Does it say anything about my ghost cat?" Val asked.

"Um . . ." Ruby ran a finger down the screen. "Here's something about the Lady in Pink. She wears a fancy ball gown and asks frightened guests if they care to dance."

"These are all just stories," Goldie said, looking over Ruby's shoulder. "There's no proof. No pictures. No video."

"What about my cat?" Val asked again.

Ruby glanced at her. "No, sorry. Nothing about a cat."

"That's okay." Val shrugged. "I saw him with my own eyes."

"We'll bring Nacho. If there's a ghost cat, he'll sniff him out." Goldie patted the top of her dog's head. She knew that unless the ghost cat was covered in maple syrup or cheese sauce, Nacho wasn't likely to find him.

"I can't wait for Saturday. You'll see, Goldie. Ghosts are real," Val said.

Goldie bit her tongue to keep from arguing *again.*

Ruby, Li, and Val left at dinnertime. Goldie stayed in the BloxShop to pack up the haunting supplies. She grabbed her duffel bag and filled it with whitening toothpaste, string, a flashlight, fishing line, pulleys, doll heads, old sheets, handheld fans, and more.

"Can you think of anything else?" she asked Nacho.

He yawned.

"I know what else we need! A witness." And Goldie knew exactly who to call.

DUMBWAITER, DUMB IDEA

Goldie's dad drove the Gearheads and Nacho to the inn late Saturday afternoon.

"You know, my first job was working in the kitchen here," he said as he pulled the car over. "I was in charge of the waffles."

Goldie nodded. That made sense. Her dad made the best waffles.

"Did you ever see any ghosts?" Val asked.

"Nope." He shook his head. "But the building did seem to be alive. Old buildings creak and moan."

They got out and thanked him for the ride.

"Are you sure you don't want me to stay with you?" he asked through an open window. "Leaving my daughter and her friends to spend the night in a haunted inn is not going to win me the father-of-the-year award."

"You're funny, Dad. It's not haunted, and we've worked it out with the town board. This is our project," Goldie explained.

Her dad waved goodbye. "Well, see you in the morning, then. Assuming you survive the night. *Bwahaha!*" He gave a spooky laugh as he drove off.

The Gearheads stood on the sidewalk in front of the inn. Even in the sunlight, the building was dark and gray. It also seemed to lean a little bit to the right, like it was sinking into the ground.

Nacho shivered.

"Ready?" Goldie asked. She carried a back-pack and her black duffel bag with supplies.

"Absolutely!" Val led them up the path. Just as they stepped onto the front porch, the door swung open.

Ruby jumped.

But it was only Zeek Zander.

"What are you doing here?" Ruby asked. She swatted away cobwebs.

"Goldie invited me." He crossed his arms and gave them a wicked smile. His expensive Butler Phone hovered nearby.

Ruby grabbed Goldie's shoulder. "Want to explain why we're hanging out with Zeek?"

The Gearheads huddled around Goldie.

"I actually invited Mayor Zander. I thought if *he* saw the ghosts, he would convince the town board to keep the place open. But the mayor had other plans, so he offered *him*." Goldie pointed to Zeek with her thumb.

"I just hope Zeek's Butler Phone doesn't scare off the ghost cat," Val said. "I really want to see it again."

Goldie turned back to Zeek. "Let's check the place out."

"After you." Zeek stepped back to let them in. "I'm only here to prove you're wrong. That's my favorite hobby."

The inside of the building was just as gloomy as the outside. What little furniture was left was covered with dusty sheets. With each step, the floor groaned.

They dropped their bags in the foyer and went to explore. The Gearheads and Zeek went to the kitchen first.

"It's so dark," Ruby said with a shiver.

"Duh, there's no electricity," Zeek said.

"But that's not a problem." Goldie pulled

back the curtains and opened the window. Yellow streaks of sun lit the room. Bugs scampered into the shadows. "That's better."

Then they went into the dining room. As they passed the bathroom, Val pushed the door open and peered inside.

"Did you see your cat?" Li asked.

"No," she whispered. "But we'll find him. I'm sure of it."

"This place is a dump," Zeek complained. He flicked the peeling wallpaper.

"It used to be beautiful," Val said.

The dining room had a wood floor in the center. Goldie could imagine people dancing here long ago. A band would be set up in the corner, and waiters in tuxedos would serve fancy food that didn't taste nearly as good as waffles or bacon.

The chandelier swung slightly. Which was

weird because there wasn't a breeze or any-thing to make it move.

"Let's go upstairs," Li said.

The second floor had twelve guest rooms. They all looked identical, with two double beds, a dresser, a closet, and a small bathroom.

"I wonder which room belonged to Funny Fred," Li said.

"Room twenty-seven," Val answered.

On the third floor, the rooms were big suites. They opened all eight doors on the third level. There were no signs of ghosts.

Goldie's eyes lit up when she noticed a small wooden door at the end of the hall.

"Look! It's the dumbwaiter." She ran to it and yanked it open. She grabbed the thick rope inside and tugged. The wooden box appeared. "I love riding in dumbwaiters. I'll go first!"

"Dumbwaiter? More like dumb *idea*," Zeek

said. "That rope is probably rotted through. But don't let me stop you from plummeting three stories."

"I'll go next," Li said.

"I'm taking the stairs," Ruby announced.

Goldie crawled inside. It was a bit tight, especially when Nacho jumped in, too. The pulleys creaked.

"I think this is a one-person-at-a-time ride, boy." She stroked her dog's head. "Well, one

person and a few spiders."

Nacho hopped out, and the pulleys stopped creaking.

Goldie tugged the rope and went down.

"Wheee," she said, even though the dumbwaiter moved very slowly. Goldie traveled down to the kitchen in total darkness. She hopped out and sent the dumbwaiter back up for Li.

No one else was in the kitchen. But she couldn't have been the first to arrive because the windows were closed and the curtains were drawn tight.

I know I opened these, she thought.

Val pushed through the swinging doors, followed by Zeek, Ruby, and Nacho.

"It's so dark in here," Ruby said. "Why did you close the windows?"

"I didn't," Goldie said. "I thought you did."

Something rustled in the corner.

Goldie couldn't see anything in the shadows. Then the dumbwaiter door flew open and Li crawled out.

"I think I prefer the laundry chute," he said. "It goes much faster but also smells much worse."

"Who closed the windows?" Ruby asked. Her voice was squeaky.

Everyone shook their heads.

"Must be ghosts." Li smiled and nudged Goldie with his elbow.

"It wasn't me or any of my special effects," she whispered to him.

"So what!" Zeck snapped. "A window closed. Could have been wind. Could have been gravity."

"Wind and gravity don't explain the curtains closing, too." Val put her hands on her hips. "But I don't think this is the work of the ghost cat. Not his style."

Goldie rolled her eyes. There had to be an explanation, but she kept quiet. Their goal was to get Zeek to believe the place was haunted.

"Let's set up the cameras," she said. "And we'll catch this ghost—or ghosts—in action."

I SCREAM

Everyone but Zeek helped arrange the five video cameras around the inn. Zeek was too busy playing a game of chess with Butler Phone.

"You win, Master Zeek," the phone said. "You have beaten me two hundred and seventeen times in a row. Want to play again?"

"Yeah," Zeek said.

Goldie pulled the Gearheads into a corner where Zeek couldn't hear them.

"I'll set up the haunted hacks." Goldie patted

her black duffel bag. "Someone needs to keep Zeek distracted. In case he gets sick of winning at chess."

"How can we distract Zeek?" Li asked.

"We'll just get him talking about himself. It's his favorite subject," Ruby suggested.

"Great. Val, will you help me set up?"

"Goldie, you don't need to do this," Val said. "This place is already—"

"I know, I know," Goldie interrupted. "This is just extra. And it'll be fun. Trust me."

"Fine." Val followed Goldie out of the kitchen to the dining room.

"Let's get our dancing shoes on," Goldie said.

"I love to dance!" Val pulled out her music player.

"But first, I need your shoes." Goldie dug in her bag until she found the whitening

toothpaste. She used a paintbrush to coat the bottom of their sneakers.

"I've never had minty-fresh shoes before," Val said as she put them back on.

"Time to dance," Goldie instructed.

They twirled and stomped across the dining room.

"I don't see anything," Val said.

"You will with this." Goldie pulled a

battery-operated lantern out of her bag. She switched the regular lightbulb for a special black-light one. She flicked the lantern on. "Ta-da. Whitening toothpaste plus a black light and you get . . ."

"Glowing footprints. That's cool," Val said.

"Just one more little touch." Goldie used the brush to write a secret message on the wall.

"What's next?" Val asked.

"The doors." Goldie walked to the entrance of the dining room. "These doors were once considered magical because if you opened one, they'd both open. They're attached with chains and pulleys under the floor." Goldie demonstrated for Val.

"What do you have planned?" Val asked.

"We're going to do something like this. We're going to connect the front door to the back door." Goldie smiled.

"I think ghosts can float through doors," Val said. "I know they can go through walls."

As they stood in the foyer, Goldie took out a spool of fishing line. A breeze blew through the large fireplace, and something rattled inside the chimney. A chill ran down Goldie's back, but she shook it off.

Goldie and Val ran the fishing line from the top of the front door, across the chandelier, around the grandfather clock, and down the hall to the back door.

"Fishing line is hard to see, especially when it's dark. That way Zeek won't know what's happening when both the doors open at once," she explained to Val.

Val and Goldie peered inside the kitchen. Ruby nodded as Zeek rattled on about all of his accomplishments. Li looked to be almost asleep.

"Then when I was in second grade, I won first place in a national calculator championship." That was all Goldie heard Zeek say before she and Val tiptoed away.

Val checked that the fishing line was tight.

"Looks good," Goldie said. "Now time for ghosts."

They ran upstairs to the second floor. Goldie opened her bag. She grabbed doll heads, sheets, string, handheld fans, and pulleys.

"These are creepier than ghosts." Val held up one of the heads.

"Just wait until we're done." Goldie showed Val how to create a ghost with her supplies. Then they hung their ghosts with string, which they ran over the pulleys and to the floor.

"Are these trip wires?" Val asked as Goldie zigzagged string across the floor.

"Yep. When Zeek walks down the hall, all

these ghosts will drop from the ceiling. It's going to be great." She clasped her hands together.

"Goldie!" Ruby called from downstairs.

Goldie and Val rushed to the stairs.

"Hurry up," Ruby whisper-yelled. "We can't keep Zeek distracted much longer. And Li is getting hungry. Every five seconds his stomach growls."

"Almost done." Goldie gave her a salute. Then she dug through her bag again. "Val, you mix the vampire slime while I place the spooky eyes in the windows." She gave Val the directions.

"Who knew haunting an inn would be so much work," Val complained. "Ghosts just have to show up. *We* have to mix slime, write spooky messages, and attach ghouls to string."

Goldie used toilet paper rolls and glow sticks to create her creepy eyes. She set them in the cloudy windows on the third floor. The whole time, she felt like someone was watching her. But when she turned around, she was still alone.

When she got back to the second floor, the vampire slime was ready to go. But there was no Val. Goldie put the bucket of slime in a wall air vent on an inclined plane. It would slowly pour into the hallway during the night.

"Goldie." Val snuck up from behind.

"Good job with the slime, Val. It's perfect. Where did you go?"

"I think I saw the cat," Val said, trying to catch her breath.

"You think?" Goldie asked.

"It was in the shadows. But something moved and meowed. I tried to catch it. But it disappeared."

Goldie shook her head. "It's an old building,

Val. There are lots of creaking noises and drafts." *But no ghost cat.* Goldie didn't say the last part. Her friend looked so hopeful.

"It wasn't a draft," Val said. "Why won't you believe me?"

Goldie ignored the question. "Come on. Let's get back to the kitchen. Zeek may have bored our friends into a coma by now." She put an arm around Val's shoulder. "And if the ghost cat is here, we'll catch him with the cameras."

Goldie picked up her duffel bag. She tried to cheer Val up with a joke. "What did the ghost eat for dessert?" she asked.

Val stayed quiet.

"I scream." Goldie chuckled. "Get it? I scream?"

Val didn't laugh.

But someone—or something—did.

It came from a guest room. The hairs on

Goldie's arms stood up.

"It's the comedian! It's Funny Fred!" Val cheered.

Goldie swallowed hard to keep terror from rising into her throat.

FIVE LETTERS. BEGINS WITH A G.

"It's not the comedian!" Goldie rubbed her arms to get rid of the goose bumps that had sprung up.

Usually, Val ran away from strange noises or any kind of danger, but now she ran toward the room where they heard the laughter.

Val flung open the door to room twenty-seven. Goldie walked up behind her.

The room was empty. Val checked under the bed and in the closet. No ghosts.

"Fred?" she called out. "Where did you go?"

"Look." Goldie pointed to a large air vent in the wall. A decorative metal grate covered it.

"You think he's in there?" Val asked. Her face wrinkled.

"No, I think sound is traveling through the air vent. It was probably the gang in the kitchen. Come on, let's go. There's no ghost here."

When they got downstairs to the kitchen, Zeek was still talking, and no one seemed to be laughing.

"By the end of third grade, I'd written two award-winning papers on the effects of electromagnetic waves on fruit flies, then—"

"We're back," Goldie interrupted.

"The torture is over!" Ruby jumped up and hugged Val and Goldie like they'd just rescued her from a toxic desert island.

"I'm starving," Li said. "What kind of kitchen doesn't have food?" He opened and closed all the cupboards.

"The kind that's been out of business for years," Val said.

"Let's order pizza," Goldie suggested. She'd packed twenty pounds of gear in her duffel bag but no snacks.

"Butler Phone, you heard her," Zeek said. "Get me some pizza."

"Yes, Master Zeek."

"And some for us, too, please," Goldie added.

While they waited for the pizza to be delivered, Goldie suggested they check out the dining room.

"Obviously, that would be a good place to eat." She nodded knowingly to Val.

The Gearheads and Zeek walked down the

hall. Ruby turned on the camera that they'd placed by the door. Goldie flicked on the black-light lantern.

"Oh my!" Goldie shrieked, trying her best to sound stunned.

The footprints glowed and so did her secret message on the wall: *Get Out! While You Still Can.*

"Awesome," Li said. He tried retracing the steps.

"What?" Zeek spun around and then laughed. "Do you really expect me to believe a ghost wrote that message? And the shoeprints? Ghosts don't walk."

"Good point, Master Zeek," Butler Phone said.

"You can't scare me. I know ghosts aren't real. And my dad owes me big-time for wasting my Saturday with you Gunkheads."

"It's Gearheads," Val corrected him.

"Whatever."

Goldie sighed. Her first haunting hadn't gone well. But she still had plenty more.

"I like the footprints, Goldie," Ruby whispered. "Will you help me put them in my room?"

"Sure."

A minute later, a car horn blared.

"Must be the pizza," Goldie said. "That was super quick."

"They know I get angry if they take too long. I *am* the son of the mayor." Zeek and Butler Phone headed to the front door.

Goldie smiled. She just knew this setup would scare them.

Zeek yanked the door open. At nearly the same instant, the back door groaned open, too. Everyone jumped, except Zeek.

"I noticed the fishing line. Who wouldn't," he sneered.

Goldie's heart sank. Maybe she couldn't convince him the place was haunted.

Zeek stepped out onto the porch to get their dinner, but the pizza delivery guy stood at the road.

"What are you doing?" Zeek asked. "Bring me my pizza."

"No way. I'm not going near that place." The delivery guy motioned with his chin at the upper floors of the inn.

The Gearheads rushed out onto the sidewalk to get a better look. They turned to see the glowing eyes that Goldie had placed in the windows.

"That's cool, too," Li whispered. "How did you do it?"

"Um . . ." She hesitated. "Glow sticks and toilet paper rolls. But . . . um . . . I only put them on the third floor." She pointed at the white eyes that came from the middle rooms. They moved and then disappeared.

Zeek, who was still on the porch, continued yelling at the pizza delivery guy. "No tip if you don't bring me my pizza. And I'm telling my dad."

"Don't care!" The delivery guy put the pizza down on the sidewalk.

"I'll get it," Li said. He grabbed the box and flipped it open. He pulled out a slice and started

eating as he carried it to the porch.

Goldie took a breath. She had goose bumps again, and it wasn't because of the cool evening air.

"You saw the eyes, didn't you?" Val said.

Goldie nodded. "There must be an explanation."

"There is. And it's simple. Five letters. Begins with a *G*," Val said.

"*Germs?*" Goldie asked.

Val groaned.

"*Girls. Glass*, like a reflection. You don't think it was a *gator*, do you?"

"What is it going to take for you to believe me?" Val huffed. Then she turned and walked back inside.

After they finished their pizza, they decided it was time to set up their sleeping bags.

"We should split up and cover as much of the inn as possible. We don't want to miss anything," Goldie said.

"That's always a bad idea," Ruby warned. "Don't you watch scary movies?"

"I'll sleep down here with Nacho." Val unrolled her sleeping bag in the middle of the foyer. "Zeek and Li can bunk on the second floor."

"Then Ruby and I will stay on the third floor," Goldie said. She needed the boys to be in a separate room so she could scare Zeek.

"Val, you don't want to stay with us?" Ruby asked, her voice shaking.

"Nope, Nacho and I will be fine."

"Okay. If you're sure." Goldie gave Nacho a hug, and then tried to give Val one, too. But Val turned away from her.

"Good night," Ruby said.

Goldie followed Ruby, Li, and Zeek upstairs. She smiled. She still had a couple of things set to scare Zeek.

"Don't step on the trip wires." Zeek pointed to the string on the ground. "We don't want to set off any more of Goldie's dorky haunted-house contraptions."

She sighed. Zeek had figured out her ghost puppets.

"We'll sleep in here," Li said. "It belonged to Funny Fred. Right?"

Goldie nodded. She didn't tell them she'd heard laughing from this room earlier. She hoped the mysterious laughter would sound again.

Li and Zeek rolled out their sleeping bags on top of the rug in the comedian's room. Dust flew through the air. Butler Phone settled onto the nightstand.

"See you in the morning," Ruby said. She turned on the camera.

Goldie and Ruby left the boys. They carefully stepped over the trip wires and around the vampire slime. It slowly oozed from the air vent.

On the third floor, Ruby turned on another camera. Then they settled into the room supposedly haunted by the Lady in Pink.

"I don't really want to see a ghost," Ruby said. "But I'm super curious about the Lady in Pink's dress. To wear the same thing for all eternity is a commitment. The outfit must be something special."

Goldie just shook her head.

A SCREAMING CUP

Goldie and Ruby sat on their sleeping bags. They each held a flashlight. Goldie had to admit, the place was a little spooky at night. But not haunted.

"This inn gives me the creeps." Ruby hugged her minicomputer to her chest like it was a teddy bear.

"You don't believe in ghosts, do you?" Goldie asked. Ruby had been quiet on the subject. She knew Val believed in ghosts, and Li wanted ghosts to be real. But Ruby had not taken a side.

"I don't know." She shrugged. "Val seems certain, and she doesn't lie. She might over-react, but she's always honest."

"I know." Goldie frowned. She could engineer contraptions and machines, but she didn't know what to do when she didn't believe in the same things as her friends. This was different from an argument. They'd had plenty of arguments. Just last week, Val had said maple syrup and butter were the best toppings for waffles. Goldie had said peanut butter, jalapeños, marshmallow fluff, and sprinkles were the best.

They'd agreed to disagree.

"I guess I'm keeping an open mind about ghosts. Mark me down as a maybe." Ruby made a check mark in the air with her finger.

"The real problem is that Zeek doesn't

think ghosts are real," Goldie said. "I can't believe I have something in common with Zeek Zander!"

"You have something else in common," Ruby said. "You both know who is haunting the inn. You! He's on to us."

"I'm not giving up yet." Goldie searched through her duffel bag and found a plastic cup, string, a paper clip, and wax.

"What's this for?" Ruby asked.

"We're going to make a screaming cup." She assembled her project and told Ruby to pinch her thumb and index finger together and slide them down the string. It made an awful noise.

Ruby grabbed her ears. "I don't know if it

sounds like a ghost. More like something being strangled and tickled at the same time."

Goldie dug through her duffel bag again. She grabbed a rubber eraser and a little robot with a one-armed vise that went up and down. She poked a hole in the tip of the eraser, then threaded it through the string. "The eraser will act like our fingers," she explained to Ruby. Then she used her screwdriver to open the air vent that led to the comedian's room. Ten minutes later, she had installed an automatic screaming machine. The robot's vise clamped down on the eraser, moving it back and forth.

Goldie and Ruby tiptoed down the stairs and through the halls, avoiding the trip wires. The door to the comedian's room was closed. Goldie used her screwdriver again to open an air vent in the hall.

"Be right back," she said to Ruby. Goldie crawled inside and placed her machine close to the comedian's room.

Then she wiggled her way back to Ruby.

"I set a timer on the robot. T-minus ten seconds until we scare Zeek into believing in ghosts."

They counted down in a whisper. The machine activated. The awful scream echoed through the entire floor of the inn. A chill ran down Goldie's back. It was worse than nails on a chalkboard.

A moment later, Li ran out of the room.

"What *is* that?" He looked around with wide eyes.

The screaming machine quieted after a few seconds.

"It was us," Goldie whispered. She explained what they had done.

"Was Zeek scared?" Ruby asked.

"I don't know." Li shrugged.

"I bet he's hiding in his sleeping bag," Goldie said. "Let's check."

Goldie pushed the door open and ran into the room. She did her best to look terrified.

"What was that? Zeek, are you okay? I think we've made the ghosts mad by being here." Goldie spoke quickly.

"Maybe we should leave this haunted inn. I'm too scared," Ruby added and winked.

But Zeek wasn't in his sleeping bag. Goldie yanked a small flashlight from her hair and shined it around the room.

"Where is he?" she asked.

"I don't know." Li checked under the beds.

Zeek had disappeared.

A second later, Nacho and Val ran into the room. Nacho went straight to Goldie. She swept

him up into a hug.

"What's going on? Did you see a ghost?" Val asked with a smile.

"No, but Zeek is missing," Goldie explained.

"He was here a minute ago," Li said. "Before the scream machine went off."

"He didn't run into the hallway," Ruby added. "We would have seen him."

There was only one other way out of the room. Li went to the window. It was jammed shut.

"No way he opened this," Li said.

"Well, he didn't just disappear," Goldie said. "We'll find him."

"We better or the mayor is going to be really upset," Val added. "He'll probably kick us out of Bloxtown."

"Wait!" An idea popped into Goldie's head. "We have video." She pointed to the camera they'd set up in the corner of the room.

Ruby grabbed it. She hooked it to her mini-computer and turned it so they could all see the screen.

The video was green and black because it was shot in the dark. Goldie had to squint to focus.

"That's us saying good night," Li explained. The video showed Li kind of waving at Zeek. Zeek fluffed his pillow and turned over. Butler Phone's glowing screen dimmed as it settled on the nightstand.

The Gearheads watched five boring minutes of Li and Zeek sleeping. Then Li jumped up. Zeek's eyes opened wide, but he didn't move. Li bolted to the door.

"That must be when you heard the scream machine," Ruby said.

Zeek grabbed Butler Phone and pulled

the sleeping bag over his head. They couldn't see him, but he was wriggling and definitely inside.

Then the video went to static.

"What's happening?" Goldie asked.

"I don't know," Ruby said. "The video cut out."

Then, suddenly, it was back on, and the room was deserted. Zeek's sleeping bag lay empty.

GHOSTS IN THE TOILET

"**A** ghost turned off the camera and snatched Zeek!" Val exclaimed.

"Stop it, Val!" Goldie snapped. "There is an explanation, and we're going to find it."

Val's shoulders dropped, and she hung her head.

"I'm sorry," Goldie mumbled. "Let's just find Zeek. Okay? That's what's important."

"I'll call Butler Phone from my mini-computer," Ruby suggested. She tapped on the screen. Her eyebrows squished together and she frowned. She tapped again.

"What's wrong?" Goldie asked.

"I can't get my computer to connect." Ruby looked up. "It's like we've been cut off from the outside world. Something weird is going on."

Goldie bit her lip. She knew internet connections got interrupted. She knew this wasn't a ghost, but she was still worried.

"It's only one a.m.," Li added. "I wonder if things will get spookier." From the way he smiled, Goldie knew that he was hoping for more.

"Let's find Zeek," Goldie said. "And let's stick together."

"A little late for that," Val mumbled.

They grabbed their flashlights. "We'll start at the bottom and work our way up."

Val led them down to the kitchen. She seemed to be the only one not shaking.

The kitchen appeared empty. Ruby checked the video and found nothing unusual. Li searched all the cupboards.

"Still no food. And no Zeek," he reported.

"This room is clear. Let's go to the dining room." Just as Goldie turned to leave, the oven door opened and then closed with a violent bang.

Ruby screamed.

"It's Chef. I know it is," Val said.

Goldie's heart jumped to her throat. Still,

she wanted to check it out. But Ruby grabbed her arm and dragged her to the dining room. Val and Li were right behind them.

"Relax. There has to be an explanation." Goldie stared at Ruby, who was pale.

"Maybe it's ghosts, Goldie," Ruby said. "And if that's true, I don't want—"

"It's not." Goldie used her flashlight again to look around the dining room. "Check under the tables for Zeek."

"Do you really think he's playing hide-and-seek with us?" Val asked.

Zeek wasn't in the dining room either. But the room was different.

"It's so cold in here," Ruby said. Her teeth chattered.

"I know." Goldie rubbed her arm.

"Ghosts like the cold," Val whispered to Goldie.

"Let's get out of here." Ruby looked around nervously.

They left the dining room. The foyer was empty. Goldie shined her flashlight up the chimney to double-check. Nothing but cobwebs. The only other room on the main floor was the bathroom.

"Allow me." Val grabbed the door handle and yanked it open. Goldie knew Val was hoping to catch the ghost cat.

No cat. No Zeek. But there was something wrong with the toilet.

"What's happening?" Ruby asked, hiding behind Li.

The water in the toilet bubbled and fizzed. The room filled with fog.

"Awesome," Li whispered.

"Not awesome!" Ruby stepped back.

"Ghosts in the toilet," whispered Val.

"Not ghosts," Goldie said. "I think we need—"

She didn't finish her sentence because she was rudely interrupted by mad laughing that echoed throughout the house. It made the walls vibrate.

The Gearheads huddled together.

"I want to go home," Ruby whispered.

Goldie did, too. But she couldn't say that out loud.

"You don't need to be afraid of ghosts," Val said calmly. She squeezed Ruby's hand.

"Take a deep breath, Gearheads. We still have the other floors to check. And I'm sure there is a logical explanation for all this." Goldie looked at Val, who seemed to understand. Because Val gave a slight nod. All the ghost talk was scaring Ruby.

They walked up the stairs in a tight group.

On the second floor, Goldie and Li took turns opening the guest room doors and checking for Zeek. They carefully stepped over the trip wires. Val held Ruby's hand as they hung back in the hallway. The Gearheads never took their eyes off each other.

"It's all clear," Goldie said. "No Zeek."

"We didn't check the dumbwaiter," Val said. She pointed to the wooden door at the end of the hall.

Goldie turned to face the dumbwaiter. As she did, something banged inside.

"What was that?" Ruby shrieked.

"Hopefully Zeek," Goldie said as she and Val marched down the hall to check it out. Li hung back with a

nervous Ruby and a terrified Nacho.

Val and Goldie put their hands on the handle at the same time. Goldie knew they were both hoping for different results.

"On the count of three?" Goldie asked.

Val nodded.

"One. Two. Three!"

DOGNAPPING

A glowing figure shot out of the dumbwaiter.

"Ghost!" Ruby yelled.

Val and Goldie ran toward their friends. They hit every trip wire they'd set up earlier. Ghost puppets dropped from the ceiling. Goldie heard screaming. She wasn't sure if it was coming from her or Val or both.

The Gearheads and Nacho bolted up the stairs. They huddled at the end of the third-floor hallway. Li kept a flashlight pointed at the

staircase. The *thing* had not followed them.

"What was that?" Goldie was the one asking this time. Ten seconds ago she hadn't believed in ghosts. But now she wasn't sure.

"It was a ghost!" Ruby said.

"Yes," Val agreed.

"Whatever it was, it was awesome," Li said.

"What do you think it was?" Val asked Goldie.

"I don't know." Her heart raced in her chest. "Maybe you're right. Maybe . . ." She couldn't finish her sentence.

Val smiled wide. Goldie tried to smile back, but she didn't have the energy.

"We need to relax and finish our search," she said. "Ghosts or no ghosts, Zeek is still missing."

They checked the rooms on the third floor. No sign of their classmate.

Ruby yawned. She had dark circles under her eyes.

"Let's get some sleep," Goldie said. "We'll have better luck in the daylight."

They gathered their sleeping bags and dragged them to the foyer. They put Ruby in the middle. Nacho curled up on Goldie's face. She gently moved him to her feet.

 "Good night, Gearheads," Goldie said. They left one flashlight on. No one wanted to be in the dark.

The old inn groaned in the night. Wind whistled through the halls. The darkness played tricks on Goldie's eyes. Something would flicker to the side, but when she turned her head, nothing was there.

Or it was gone.

She somehow fell asleep for a little bit. But

when she woke, it wasn't morning yet. She looked over at her friends.

Ruby's eyes were shut tight. Goldie knew she wasn't sleeping because her face wasn't relaxed. It was all scrunched up.

"Ruby, there's nothing to be afraid of," Goldie whispered. "It's just—"

Before she finished her thought, Nacho jumped to his paws. His ears stood up.

"What is it, boy?" Goldie asked.

He stared into the hallway. He growled. He barked.

Then something small and white shot through the room.

"Meooooow!"

Nacho chased it up the stairs.

"Come back, Nacho!" Goldie yelled.

"Come back, ghost cat!" Val yelled.

They scrambled out of their sleeping bags

and ran after the animals. Goldie took the stairs two at a time, but Val was faster. Still, four legs beat two legs. Nacho and the ghost cat raced to the third floor and out of sight.

"Where did they go?" Val asked. She opened and closed doors to the empty rooms.

"Nacho! Come back, boy! Nacho!"

Li and Ruby joined them on the third floor.

"Was that really the ghost cat?" Li asked.

"Yes!" Val said.

"No," Goldie said.

"We all saw it." Val crossed her arms.

"Did you notice the blue glow of the ghost cat?" Goldie asked.

"I did," Ruby said. "It was so creepy."

Li nodded.

"It didn't have a creepy glow because it was a ghost," Goldie said. "It was the glow from a device. An LED screen."

"What device flies and has a glowing screen?" Val asked. She paused. Then the answer hit her. "Butler Phone," she mumbled.

"Huh? Why would Butler Phone pretend to be a ghost?" Li asked.

Goldie shrugged. "Zeek must be trying to scare *us*. He wants us to think the place is haunted."

"But we're trying to do the same thing," Ruby said. "Why would he be behind all this?"

"I don't know. But we're going to find out. And we're going to find Nacho." Goldie led the gang back to the kitchen. She pulled open the oven door. Inside she found a small motorized door opener.

She yanked it out. "Our ghost Chef is just an automatic door opener on a timer."

Li moved in for a closer look. "Like what stores use to open and shut their glass doors."

"Yep. Looks like he adjusted it to slam."
Goldie put it on the counter. This little mechanism wasn't cheap. "And I bet the cold dining room is just a small air conditioner."

They went to check it out, and Goldie was right. They found the unit under a few broken boards in the dance floor.

"What about the bubbly toilet?" Val asked. Goldie could hear the hope in her voice.

"Probably dry ice," Goldie said. "Drop a

hunk of dry ice in warm water, and you get fog. Lots of it. It's really kind of cool, but not good for pipes." They went to check it out. But the toilet water had calmed down. The dry ice had melted.

"And the ghost on the second floor that flew out of the dumbwaiter?" Val asked.

"Probably just a hologram," Li said. "The expensive kind. It was an impressive ghost. Don't ya think?"

"So Zeek's behind all this. But why? And where did he go?" Ruby asked.

"Let's head back to the scene of the crime," Goldie said. "Not that there's been a crime. Except for dognapping Nacho."

In the comedian's room, everything was how they'd left it. Goldie took her flashlight and crawled into Zeek's sleeping bag headfirst.

"What are you doing?" Ruby asked Goldie's

feet. They were the only part of her sticking out.

"Looking for clues," Goldie shouted. A moment later, she popped out with a remote in her hand.

"That's how he controlled the camera," Ruby said.

"But where did he go?" Val asked.

"We know he didn't go out the door, because Ruby and I were waiting in the hall," Goldie said.

"He didn't go out the window. I checked. It's stuck," Li reminded them.

"And he wasn't evaporated by ghosts," Val mumbled, sounding disappointed.

"So how else can someone get out of this room?" Ruby asked.

"Maybe he didn't get out," Goldie suggested.

"Do you think he's still here?" Ruby whispered.

"Not exactly. He hid somewhere until we left. Then he snuck out." Goldie waved for her friends to follow her into the hallway.

"So we're back to the start. He could be anywhere," Val said.

"No. There may be another clue. Wait here." Goldie ran to the dining room and grabbed her black-light lantern.

"Watch this." She turned on the light. The vampire slime Val had created lit up half the hallway. And beyond that, there were footprints. Zeek's footprints.

"He stepped in the goo," Goldie explained. They followed the footprints to the janitor's closet and then to the laundry chute.

"He's in the basement," Goldie said.

Li pulled open the chute door. "Anyone care to go for a ride?"

JUST THE AUTUMN WIND

Goldie jumped into the laundry chute first. She slid on her bottom all the way to the basement. She tumbled into a basket of dusty rags. Then Ruby landed on her. They got out of the way before Li and Val could crash on top of them.

The laundry room was small and bare. Still no Zeek or Nacho. But a faint light glowed under the door that led to the rest of the basement. Goldie quietly pushed it open.

Zeek sat at a laptop with Butler Phone

hovering right behind him. Nacho slept in the corner in a laundry basket. An empty box of maple-flavored dog biscuits lay next to him. But what surprised Goldie was that Zeek, Butler Phone, and Nacho were not alone. Someone was standing next to Zeek.

"Mayor Zander, what are you doing here?" she asked in her loudest voice.

Mayor Zander and Zeek both jumped.

"I'm just . . . I wanted to make sure . . . um, there was no funny business." The mayor straightened his bow tie.

"Funny business?" Li asked. "You mean all the tricks that Zeek has been up to?"

"I didn't do anything!" Zeek yelled.

"The oven? The sounds? The toilet? We know it's you," Val said. "Goldie figured it all out."

Zeek pointed a finger at Goldie. "And

you were behind the slime and the screechy noises."

"We needed to convince you the inn was haunted," Goldie said.

"And we needed to convince *you* that the inn was haunted," Zeek shot back.

"But why?" Val asked.

"This doesn't make any sense," Ruby added. "It's like we're on the same team."

Mayor Zander adjusted his bow tie again and then cleaned his glasses. He seemed to be stalling.

Goldie stared at the bow tie. She knew she was missing something.

"You've all made a mess of things," the mayor said, still pulling on his bow tie.

"I got it!" Goldie yelled. "I know why you want us to think the inn is haunted. You don't want this place destroyed either. It means something to you. That boy in the picture with his lemonade stand was *you*. You were wearing that big bow tie!"

"I don't know what you're talking about," he grumbled.

Li, Val, and Ruby squinted hard at the mayor.

"It's him," Li agreed. "You're right, G."

"No . . . I . . . It's not . . . ," the mayor stammered.

"Give up, Dad," Zeek said. "It's over."

"Fine," Mayor Zander admitted. "I made my first buck selling lemonade on the front porch. That was my first business. Zander's Lemonade.

 By the end of that summer, I had three locations and six kids working for me. So yes, this place means something to me."

"It's also where he met

my mother," Zeek added.

"That, too." The mayor shrugged.

"Why didn't you just tell the town board that they can't destroy the inn?" Ruby asked. "It would have saved us a lot of trouble."

"I don't want them thinking I'm emotional and caring. I'm a businessman and the mayor." He puffed out his chest. "And no one is going to tell them otherwise."

"So what do we do now?" Ruby asked. "Do we all lie and say we've seen the ghosts of the inn?"

"I have a better idea," Goldie said.

"What?" asked Zeek.

Goldie smiled. "Think of it as a business opportunity." She explained her plan to the Zanders and the Gearheads. They all liked it and agreed to share it with the town board on Monday.

Li yawned. Then everyone else did, too. The sun peeked through the cloudy windows of the basement.

"We stayed up all night," Ruby said.

"Yep. Except Nacho." Goldie nudged her dog awake. "Time to go home and take a nap."

Zeek and Mayor Zander went up the stairs first. Li and Ruby followed. Only Val, Goldie, and Nacho were left.

"I'm sorry we didn't see any ghosts," Goldie said to her friend. "I don't believe in them, but that doesn't mean I don't believe in you. If you ever want to go ghost hunting again, I'll be there with you. Haunted mansions. Haunted caves. Haunted factories. Haunted playgrounds. Anywhere. I'll go."

"I know, Goldie." Val smiled. "That's what makes you an awesome friend. You're always willing to look for trouble."

They laughed.

"But I don't think I'll be hunting for ghosts again," Val continued.

"You don't believe anymore?" Goldie asked.

Val shook her head. "I didn't say that."

Goldie raised her eyebrows and hoped Val would explain. But she didn't. Goldie carried Nacho up the stairs.

"You coming?" she asked Val.

"Be there in a second."

Goldie stood at the top of the stairs.

"Where's Val?" Ruby asked. "She didn't disappear. Did she?"

"No." Goldie leaned her head toward the basement. She could hear Val's voice, but she couldn't make out the words. Two minutes later, Val walked up the steps.

"Who were you talking to?" Goldie asked.

Val shrugged. "No one you would know."

A cold breeze blew through Goldie's hair.
Goose bumps covered her skin.

It's just the autumn wind, she thought.

NACHO AS GHOST CAT

The town board loved Goldie's idea of turning the Bloxtown Inn into a Halloween attraction. So of course, Mayor Zander took all the credit.

"I'm a business genius!" he boomed as they stood in front of the old inn.

Ruby sold tickets to the scariest building in the entire state. People were lined up around the block to get in.

Li, Zeek, and Goldie had arranged haunted hacks on every floor. There had been some disagreement. Goldie and Li

wanted to reuse her original hacks. Zeek had wanted to order robot monsters and special effects from Hollywood. In the end, they'd compromised. They used the glow-in-the-dark footprints, the vampire slime, and the scream machine. Zeek bought one small monster. But it was so scary, he sent it back.

It was Val's job to lead the tours. She told the ghost stories about Funny Fred, the Chef, and the Lady in Pink. But everyone's favorite was Val's own story of seeing the ghost cat when she was a little girl. And then seeing it again not too long ago.

"I was visiting the inn with my best friends. They didn't believe in ghosts and spirits. They thought all could be explained with science." Val led a group through the dim hallway. The only light came from the flashlight she carried.

"But there was a moment when I was

alone, where I could be quiet and still. The cat appeared to me again. Just like it had when I was a little girl. And I spoke to it."

"What did you say?" a boy in the crowd asked.

"I told the cat that she was safe and this would always be her home. And that I was bringing more friends for her to see. You are those friends." Val motioned to the tourists.

Suddenly, behind her, a cat meowed and then streaked from the kitchen into the bath-room.

People gasped and jumped. Goldie smiled. Nacho was getting good at playing the role of the ghost cat. He was born for the part.

"Let's move into the kitchen," Val said, continuing the tour.

Goldie didn't follow. She wanted to check on the contraptions and mechanisms on the

second floor. She needed to make certain they were working. Goldie turned to the stairs. Sleeping on the bottom step was Nacho.

"Then what was in the hall?" she mumbled. *A ghost? No way.*

She couldn't explain it. And maybe she never would. But having good friends and a little mystery in her life made Goldie the happiest girl in Bloxtown.

HAUNTED HACKS

Want to hack Halloween just like Goldie Blox? Make your own spooky scares with these spine-chilling inventions from the GoldieBlox YouTube series, *Hack Along with GoldieBlox*! For more supercool DIYs, subscribe to the GoldieBlox channel!

SCREAMING CUP

Materials

A paper clip

1 large plastic cup

24 inches of string

Violin wax or rosin

Fun decorations

Directions

1. Use the paper clip to poke a hole in the bottom of the cup that's just large enough to thread a piece of string through.
2. Thread the string through the hole and tie a knot at the end of the string inside the cup to hold it in place.
3. Coat the string with violin wax or rosin. (If you don't have either, you can just use water to wet the string.)
4. Holding the cup in one hand, use your other hand to pinch the string between your thumb and forefinger.
5. Squeeze the string tightly and slide your thumb and forefinger down it to create a screaming sound.
6. Decorate your cup however you'd like! Add googly

eyes and make teeth out of construction paper to create a creepy monster, or add glitter, beads, and feathers to make it fancy.

How does the screaming cup work?

Sliding your fingers down the string makes sound vibrations. The violin wax makes the string sticky and increases those vibrations. The cup amplifies the sound, which makes it sound like it's screaming.

GLOW-STICK EYES

Materials

Toilet paper roll	Craft knife
Black paper tape	Glow stick

Directions

1. Cover the toilet paper roll with black paper tape.
2. Cut spooky eye shapes in the toilet paper roll using the craft knife.
3. Snap the glow stick to activate it and place it in the roll.
4. Cover the ends of the roll with black paper tape.

How do glow sticks work?

Inside glow sticks are two compartments filled with chemical solutions. When you snap those compartments, the solutions combine and react to create a glowing effect.

Goldie Blox.

ROLL UP YOUR SLEEVES AND GET READING!

Collect all the books in the series!

GOLDIE BLOX AND THE THREE DARES

GOLDIE BLOX AND THE BEST! PET! EVER!

GOLDIE BLOX RUINS RULES THE SCHOOL!

GOLDIE BLOX AND THE HAUNTED HACKS!

31901063518718

1340